Wiggle-Waggle WOOF!

Dedicated to mushers everywhere ~ and for all those
who have a special place in their hearts for wet noses
and wagging tails.

To Lance Mackey ~ Thank you for your kindness.

To Scott ~ "olives"
—CHÉRIE B. STIHLER

To red-headed Patton, you snuck into our lives, into our hearts, and into this book!
—MICHAEL BANIA

Manufactured in China in November 2015 by C&C Offset Printing Co. Ltd. Shenzhen, Guangdong Province
Published by Sasquatch Books
18 17 16   9 8 7 6 5

Cover design: Michael Bania
Interior design: Rosebud Eustace
Editor: Michelle Roehm McCann

Library of Congress Cataloging-in-Publication Data is available.

ISBN-13: 978-1-57061-559-7
ISBN-10: 1-57061-559-4

Sasquatch Books
1904 Third Avenue, Suite 710
Seattle, WA 98101
(206) 467-4300
www.sasquatchbooks.com
custserv@sasquatchbooks.com

Wiggle-Waggle WOOF!

Counting Sled Dogs in Alaska

 Chérie B. Stihler

 Illustrations by Michael Bania

 PAWS IV *published by* SASQUATCH BOOKS

One dog truck

DOG TRUCK

A truck or van with added spaces (called "dog boxes") for transporting dogs and supplies

Rattle-rattle, clang-clang

Two little noses

Sniff-sniff-sniff

Three dogs wait.
Soon it will be their turn.

Wiggle-waggle, wiggle-waggle,

WOOF!
WOOF!
WOOF!

Four paws prance,
Left-right, left-right

Five heads bob
Swing dogs bark

SWING DOGS
The dogs right behind the lead
dogs; they also help steer

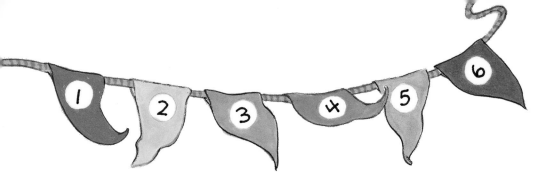

Six eyes watch
Hooking up the wheel dogs

Wiggle-waggle,
wiggle-waggle,
WOOF! WOOF! WOOF!

WHEEL DOGS
The dogs closest to the sled

Seven in harness

Jingle-jingle, jing-jang

Eight on neck-lines

Stretch

Scratch

Snoooze

NECK-LINE
Connects a dog collar to the tow-line

Nine booties
fall off.
Put them back on—
QUICK!

BOOTIES

Small polar-fleece socks that fit
over dog paws to protect from
jagged rocks and ice; booties
close with Velcro-style tabs

Wiggle-waggle, wiggle-waggle,

Ten ears flopping

Flip-flap, flip-flop

Eleven tails wagging

Swish Swish

Swish

TUG-LINE

Connects the back of a dog's
harness to the tow-line

Twelve on tug-lines
Soon it will be time to go!

Wiggle-waggle, wiggle-waggle,

WOOF! WOOF! WOOF!

Thirteen huskies howl

Ruff! Ruff! Aroooo!

Fourteen dogs hitched
Ready to go!

Fifteen heads turn
Waiting for the countdown

5 Five **4** Four **3** Three

2
Two

1
One

They're off!

MUSHING LINGO

DOG TRUCK

A truck or van with added spaces (called "dog boxes") for transporting dogs and supplies

MUSHER

A person who enjoys dog mushing; most likely comes from the French verb "marcher," which means "to walk"

BOOTIES

Small polar-fleece socks that fit over dog paws to protect from jagged rocks and ice; booties close with Velcro-style tabs

NECK-LINE

Connects a dog collar to the tow-line

TOW-LINE

Runs up between the dogs and connects them to the sled; tug-lines and neck-lines attach to the tow-line

LEAD DOGS

The dogs at the front of a team; they steer and let the other dogs know how fast to run

WHEEL DOGS

The dogs closest to the sled

SWING DOGS

The dogs right behind the lead dogs; they also help steer

TUG-LINE

Connects the back of a dog's harness to the tow-line

More About MUSHING

MORE MUSHING LINGO:

GEE: Turn right

HAW: Turn left

HIKE: Go

WHOA: Stop

The most famous sled dog races in the United States are:

THE IDITAROD: A 1,000-mile dogsled race from Anchorage to Nome, a portion of which follows the historic Seward-to-Nome Mail Trail, which is sometimes referred to as the Iditarod Trail.

THE YUKON QUEST: A 1,110-mile international race from Fairbanks, Alaska, to Whitehorse, Yukon Territory, Canada.

The first musher to win both the Yukon Quest and the Iditarod in the same year was Lance Mackey. He has accomplished this amazing feat more than once.

The average team speed of a top-finishing dog team is around eight to twelve miles per hour.

During a race, each dog should eat about ten thousand calories per day. That is like eating twenty-five peanut butter sandwiches for lunch.

For a long race (like the Iditarod or the Yukon Quest), a team of fourteen dogs needs about one thousand booties. That is about one set of four booties per day, per dog.

Extra dog booties, dog and musher food, and fresh bales of straw are dropped at the checkpoints along the race route for each team. Mushers use about one bale of straw for their teams each time they stop for a rest. The straw is bunched up like a large cushion on the snow for each dog to have a warm, dry, and snuggly spot to sleep.

At checkpoints, mushers first take care of their dog teams. Dogs are fed and watered. They are checked to make sure that they are healthy and happy. Then mushers make up all the beds and tuck in each dog with a dog blanket or jacket. Only once the dogs are resting will mushers make sled repairs and grab a small meal or a nap for themselves.

The "Red Lantern" is an honor given to the last musher who finishes a race. Long ago, roadhouses put a lantern outside for travelers to see their destination and to let others know that a musher was still out on the trail. Lamps were left out until an expected musher arrived at the roadhouse. The lantern is a symbol of safe passage for all mushers.